Library
Library

For the children of Waverley Primary School.
— G.S.

To Paula, Emily, Eunice,
and all the other children who love reading books,
with all my affection.
— F.C.

First published in Great Britain in 2011 by
Gullane Children's Books
185 Fleet Street, London, EC4A 2HS
www.gullanebooks.com

This edition published in 2011 by Eerdmans Books for Young Readers,
an imprint of Wm. B. Eerdmans Publishing Co.
2140 Oak Industrial Dr. NE, Grand Rapids, Michigan 49505
P.O. Box 163, Cambridge CB3 9PU U.K.

www.eerdmans.com/youngreaders

Manufactured at Shenzhen Fuweizhi Printing Ltd., in China, March 2011, first edition

17 16 15 14 13 12 11   8 7 6 5 4 3 2 1

Library of Congress Cataloging-in-Publication Data

Shields, Gillian.
Library Lily / Gillian Shields; illustrated by Francesca Chessa.
p. cm.
Summary: From the day her mother introduces her to the library, Lily wants to spend all of her time reading until she meets Milly, who hates reading but loves adventure.
ISBN 978-0-8028-5401-8 (alk. paper)
[1. Books and reading — Fiction. 2. Play — Fiction. 3. Best friends — Fiction. 4. Friendship — Fiction. 5. Libraries — Fiction.] I. Chessa, Francesca, ill. II. Title.
PZ7.S55478Lib 2011
[E] — dc22
2010053737

Library Lily

Gillian Shields

illustrated by
Francesca Chessa

Eerdmans Books for Young Readers
Grand Rapids, Michigan • Cambridge, U.K.

When Lily learned to read, her mom was very pleased.
She took Lily to the library and got her a library card.

Lily was so excited. There were
fat books, thin books, great enormous square books,
old books, new books, and furry-touchy-feely books.

Going to the library was like going on an adventure.

THIS WAY
MY LITTLE DOG BOOK
MY BIG CAT BOOK
Lily's library card

The trouble was, once Lily started to read, she couldn't stop.

She read at night
under the blankets.

...and the great
sea monster rose up
from the waves...

"Lily!" said Mom.
"Aren't you asleep yet?!"

She read in the
morning when she was
brushing her teeth.

...the rare lesser
Amazonian snake
lays its eggs...

"I need the bathroom, Lily!"

When her dinner was
ready, she forgot to eat.

...until that moment,
I, Herbert Wobble-Smythe,
had never seen a ghost...

"Lily, please eat up!"

And when her mom
spoke to her,
she just didn't hear.

...long, long ago, far,
far away, there was
once a perfect...

"Oh, Lily . . ." laughed Mom.

Lily read and read and read.

"There goes Library Lily,"
people began to say.
"Always has her head in a book."

Lily read all the way through
a sizzling summer . . .

an awesome autumn . . .

and a wonderful winter.

And when spring came around again . . .

she didn't notice.
She was in a beautiful dream. She was reading.

One sunny morning,
Lily's mom took her to the park.
"Why don't you go and play?" Mom asked.

"But I want to finish my story," said Lily.
"It's such an exciting adventure."
"Maybe you'll have an adventure in the park," smiled Mom.

So Lily wandered over to the playground . . .

WELCOME TO
THE PARK

NO DOGS
ON THE SWINGS

CIRCUS
COMING
SOON

. . . and read the signs.

That didn't take long.

She was just wondering what else she could find to read, when someone called out.

"Hey! What are you doing?"
"Reading, of course!" said Lily.
"Reading's boring!" said the upside-down voice.
"In fact, I hate reading."

"**Hate reading!**" gasped Lily.
"What DO you like?"

"Lots of things!" the upside-down person said.
"Playing. Climbing. Exploring."

"I'm Milly," said Milly.

"I'm Lily," said Lily.

Milly grinned.
"Would you like to climb my tree?"

Lily scrambled up the tree to join Milly.
From the top, they could see the green park, the busy streets, the library, and the town, all spread out below them like a picture.

"Wow!" breathed Lily.

"There's a whole world out there," said Milly.
"There's a whole world in here too,"
exclaimed Lily, pulling a book from her bag.

"You'll see!"

And so, all summer long,
Milly took Lily exploring.
It was fun!

Lily took Milly on adventures too.
Milly decided that books weren't boring
after all. They were great!

And what was extra special

was doing everything

together!

"There goes Library Lily,"

people began to say.
"With her best friend

Milly."

"What shall we do when we grow up?" said Lily to her best friend one day.

"Be explorers!" said Milly.

"There's a WHOLE WORLD out there!"

So that's exactly what they did.

And when they came home again,
Lily wrote down all their adventures . . .

. . . in the most
marvelous, magical, amazing,
PERFECT BOOK!
(You might just find it in your library!)

The Adventur
Lily and Mil